The End of the Beginning

The End of the Beginning

Being the Adventures of a Small Snail

(and an Even Smaller Ant)

AVI

WITH ILLUSTRATIONS BY
TRICIA TUSA

Harcourt, Inc.

Orlando   Austin   New York   San Diego   London

Requests for permission to make copies of any part of the work should be
submitted online at www.harcourt.com/contact or mailed to the following address:
Permissions Department, Houghton Mifflin Harcourt Publishing Company,
6277 Sea Harbor Drive, Orlando, Florida 32887-6777.

www.HarcourtBooks.com

First Harcourt paperback edition 2008

A substantially different version of this story was previously published as
Snail Tale: The Adventures of a Rather Small Snail by Pantheon Books in 1972.

The Library of Congress has cataloged the hardcover edition as follows:
Avi, 1937–
The end of the beginning: being the adventures of a small snail
(and an even smaller ant)/Avi; illustrated by Tricia Tusa.
p. cm.
Summary: Avon the snail and Edward, a take-charge ant, set off together on a
journey to an undetermined destination in search of unspecified adventures.
[1. Voyages and travels—Fiction. 2. Adventure and adventurers—Fiction.
3. Snails—Fiction. 4. Ants—Fiction. 5. Insects—Fiction.] I. Tusa, Tricia, ill.
II. Title.
PZ7.A953Ep 2004
[E]—dc22   2004002696
ISBN 978-0-15-204968-3
ISBN 978-0-15-205532-5 pb

Text set in Mrs. Eaves
Designed by Judythe Sieck

C E G H F D B

Printed in the United States of America

To Avon from Edward, with surprise

CHAPTER ONE

In Which the Adventure Begins

Avon, a rather small snail, read a book every day. He loved to read because books told him all about the things that creatures did when they went on adventures.

Now, Avon had noticed that when creatures finished their adventures, and when the stories ended, the creatures were always happy. Because Avon had never had an adventure of his own, the more he read, the sadder he became. It was absolutely necessary, he decided, to have adventures for himself. Only then would he be happy.

He sighed. "No adventures will ever come my way."

A newt who was passing by overheard Avon's words. "Nay, lad, don't say such things."

"But don't you see," said Avon, close to tears, "the most important thing in the world is having adventures. Not only have I not had any, I don't think I ever will. And if I don't have adventures—like the ones I've read about in these books—I'm bound to be unhappy forever."

"Then go out and seek some adventures," said the newt.

"I don't know how," Avon said.

"Remember, lad," said the newt, "if it's going to be tomorrow, it might as well be today. And if it is today, it could have been yesterday. If it *was* yesterday, then you're over and done with it, and can write your own book. Think about that."

Avon thought about it for a long moment, and then he said right out loud,

"Yes, I will do it. Yesterday for sure!"

CHAPTER TWO

In Which Avon Gets Some Advice

Avon began to prepare for his adventures by putting his house in proper order, certain that if he did not leave right away, he might never go. Then, just as he was about to close the door, he heard a voice.

"Not going off without saying good-bye, are you?"

It was an ant.

"I've been living here," said the ant, "for a whole year, and you have never once said hello."

"I am sorry," replied Avon. "But there was never anyone around to introduce us."

"I kept telling myself you were just being polite," said the ant. "And I'm glad to learn I was right. Still, if you have ever noticed, while it's awkward to say hello without introductions, one can always say good-bye."

"Now that you mention it, I have noticed," said Avon. "When one sets out on a journey such as I'm about to take, it's necessary to notice everything."

"What sort of a journey is it?" asked the ant.

Avon told the ant all about his plan to seek adventures. "Of course," said Avon, "I've never done anything like this before, so if you have any suggestions, I would be happy to hear them."

A worried look came upon the ant's face. "Do you mean to tell me you don't really know what sort of journey you're going on?"

"I'm afraid not," said Avon.

"Hmmmm," said the ant. "You'll need a lot of questions answered."

"Might you have the answers?"

"Well," said the ant, "if I don't have a right answer, at least I'll have a wrong one."

"As long as it's an answer," said Avon, "I can use it. You absolutely must come with me."

"I'd very much like to," confessed the ant. "If I do, however, there won't be anybody for you to say good-bye to. Half the fun of going away is saying good-bye."

"There, you see!" exclaimed Avon. "If you weren't here, I would have gone without saying good-bye to anyone."

"I suggest that you say good-bye to me,"

said the ant. "Then leave. After a few moments, I'll come along and we can go on together."

Avon readily agreed.

"Only let's get it over with," said the ant. "I really hate long good-byes."

"Good-bye, Ant," began Avon. "Don't spend any time worrying about me. Have a pleasant time, do lots of work, get plenty of exercise. I'll let you know when I'm coming back."

"Good-bye, Snail. I do hope you have some exciting adventures. Take care of yourself, have a good time, and don't forget to write."

With tears in his eyes, Avon shut the door and started on his adventures.

The ant waited for a few minutes, then skitted out to join Avon, who had set off down the branch.

"By the way," said Avon, as they began to move slowly along together, "do you have a name?"

"As a matter of fact, I do. It's Edward."

"My name is Avon."

Edward reached out to shake hands with Avon, but when he realized Avon did not have hands, he shook one of his own. "Pleased to meet you," he said.

CHAPTER THREE

In Which Music Is Introduced

Avon and Edward had gone about three inches when Edward said, "Avon, what do you know about music?"

"Oh, nothing more than a few tunes, most of which I've forgotten."

Edward was concerned. "In looking for adventures," he explained, "one does a lot of marching. It's unheard of to have adventures without marching music."

"I'm glad you warned me, Edward. Perhaps you could teach me some."

"Delighted," said Edward. "This is a very ancient marching song that has been sung in my family for thousands of years. It goes like this:

> "*March, march*
> *Golly, golly, golly.*
> *March, march*
> *Golly, golly, golly.*
> *March, march*
> *Oh, golly, golly, golly, oh.*
> *Oh, oh, oh,*
> *Oh, golly, golly, golly, oh.*
> *Oh, golly, golly, golly, oh.*
> *March, march, march!*"

"What an inspiring song," said Avon.

"One of the better things about it," Edward pointed out, "is the fact that it can be sung from either end. I sing it from the beginning, and my father sings it from the end."

"Can it be sung from the middle?"

"Absolutely," said Edward. "That's how

my mother always does it. As you can see, we are a family of individuals."

"Ah, but at least you're all singing the same song," said Avon.

CHAPTER
FOUR

In Which Edward Becomes Exhausted

Not long after Avon and Edward had set off on their adventures, Edward suddenly stopped. "I can't go on this way," he announced.

Avon became alarmed. "What's the matter?"

"My knees hurt," replied Edward, sitting down and panting. "I had no idea it would be so exhausting to go so slowly," he explained.

Avon began to feel guilty. "Is it wrong to go slow?"

"It's not wrong," said Edward, "it's just that you *take* such a long time."

Avon was embarrassed. "I know," he said softly. "It's much better for creatures to give than to take."

"It's very kind of you to offer to give me some of your time," said Edward, "but frankly, Avon, I don't think you have any to spare. You seem to need a great deal of it."

Avon was very upset. "What are we going to do, then?"

All of a sudden Edward leaped up and

ran. He ran so fast and far that Avon lost sight of him for three days and three nights.

At last, however, Edward returned, lay down, and closed his eyes.

"Are you feeling better?" Avon asked as carefully as possible.

"Not at all," answered Edward, breathing hard.

"Why, what happened?"

"I ran about in every possible direction."

"Wasn't it interesting?"

"Actually," said Edward, "no matter how fast I went, or where I went, all I saw were branches and leaves. The truth is, it wasn't very different *there* . . . than . . . *here*."

"Edward, you needn't worry about that,"

said Avon sympathetically. "As far as I can see, I don't get anywhere, either."

"True," said Edward. "I rushed off and you stayed put. But, nevertheless, we're both here."

"What's more," said Avon, "it took the same amount of time for both of us to get there."

CHAPTER FIVE

In Which the Adventurers Get Lost

It was raining very hard on the branch—so hard that Avon and Edward were having difficulties getting on. Edward kept racing ahead, ducking under a leaf, and waiting for Avon to catch up.

"Have you any idea how long this journey is going to take?" asked Edward.

Avon stopped suddenly. *"Me?"* he asked.

"I thought *you* were leading the way."

Edward was upset. "Great," he announced. "We're lost."

Avon felt like crying. "I'm sorry, Edward. My mind is on any adventures that might come along. I wasn't paying particular attention to where we were going."

"There, there," said Edward, realizing he had hurt Avon's feelings. "Getting yourself lost is easy. Happens *all* the time. It's finding yourself that's hard. So, I suggest we stop at the first door we come to and ask for suggestions."

"You mean *directions,* don't you?"

"It's hard enough being lost," explained Edward, "but worse still if you don't know what you're lost from. So, suggestions first, directions second."

It wasn't long before they came to a door, upon which they knocked. After a while they heard some steps and then a tiny voice.

"Who is it?"

"It's Avon and Edward."

"Do I know you?" asked the voice.

"I don't think so."

"Is there anyone out there who knows you?" asked the voice.

Avon said, "Edward here is a very good friend of mine. Do you want to speak to him?"

"Does anyone know him?"

"I consider myself his best friend," said Avon.

"Oh, well," said the voice. "With so many friends, you both must be quite nice." Opening the door, the voice revealed herself to be an old salamander. Urging the travelers to come in out of the rain, she led them to her kitchen, where they could warm themselves before a fire. Once they were settled down with hot drinks and cookies, she asked what had brought them to her door.

"Well," said Edward, reaching for another cookie, "we wanted to know if this was the right road."

"I think," said the salamander, "that depends on which particular place you are going to."

"We hadn't decided," said Avon.

"In that case," said the salamander, "you'll want to continue down the branch until the first turning, then go to the left."

"What's that way?" inquired Edward.

"I don't know," she replied. "I've never been that way myself. But I have been every other way and I can assure you, *they* all lead to particular places."

Edward took a sip of tea. "Then that certainly sounds like the way we should go."

By the time they finished their snack, it had stopped raining, and the two friends were anxious to start. They thanked the salamander for her hospitality.

"No bother at all," she said. "But, boys, promise me one thing. If you know you are going to be lost again, do let me know ahead of time. Then I'll have a proper supper prepared for you."

"Madam," said Avon, "believe me, the next time we don't know where we are, we shall come right here."

CHAPTER
SIX

In Which Dragons Are Mentioned

Edward," said Avon, "do you think we'll meet up with a dragon one of these days? Our travels won't be much of an adventure if we don't."

"I must warn you," said Edward, "nowadays dragons are rather shy. They disguise themselves to look like other creatures. You'll see when we meet one. They deny it every time. As a rule, though, I would say that good dragons disguise themselves as nice creatures, and bad dragons as nasty ones."

"It's a good thing you told me that," said Avon. "I've been looking for dragons. Now I'll look for something else, since I do indeed want to see one."

Edward nodded. "My father used to say, 'Edward, it's better to look for nothing and find something than to look for something and find nothing.'"

"I'll keep a sharp lookout," said Avon.

"A look *in* might be useful, too," said Edward.

Avon suddenly stopped. "Look!" he

cried. "That may be a dragon!"

Curled up by a leaf was a young, sleeping mouse.

"He certainly doesn't look like a dragon, does he?" asked Avon.

"That means he probably is one," said Edward.

The two friends crept cautiously toward the mouse.

"What a wonderful disguise!" exclaimed Avon. "I never would have guessed he was a dragon."

The mouse began to stir.

"Now, be careful," warned Edward. "We don't know yet if he's a good dragon or a bad one."

The mouse opened his eyes and saw Avon and Edward looking at him. "I beg your pardon," he said.

"We didn't mean to wake you," said Avon. "We're on our adventures, and we wanted to see a dragon."

"A dragon?" said the mouse shyly. "I'm afraid you won't find one here."

Edward nudged Avon. Avon nodded.

"You can't fool us," said Edward. "You're a dragon."

The mouse looked himself over.

"We won't tell anyone your secret," Avon said gently.

"I do hate to disappoint you, sirs," said the mouse, "but really, I am not a dragon."

"You have a tail, don't you?" asked Edward.

The mouse had to admit that.

"There," said Avon triumphantly. "Dragons have tails."

"And four feet," said Edward. "You do have four feet."

"Same as dragons," put in Avon.

"And a nose, a mouth, and two eyes!" cried Edward. "All just like a dragon. No sir, Mister Dragon, you can fool some creatures, but you can't fool Avon and Edward."

"Do you know," whispered the astonished mouse, "my father never told me I was a dragon."

"Ask your mother," suggested Edward.

"You'll have to excuse me," said the mouse, who was by then quite excited. "This is all very sudden to me. I need to go home and tell my friends who I am." And off he ran.

"Oh dear," said Avon as the mouse scampered away. "We forgot to find out if he was a good or a bad dragon."

"He was young," said Edward, "so he probably hasn't made up his mind."

"I do hope he decides to become a good dragon," said Avon. "The world needs more good dragons."

"It would certainly be a comfort," said Edward.

CHAPTER SEVEN

In Which a Battle Is Fought

Edward and Avon came to a fork in their branch.

"It seems to me," said Edward, "that you won't have had a proper series of adventures unless you've gone through thick and thin."

"Thick and thin what?" asked Avon.

"Branches," replied Edward. "We've been

on a thick branch; it's time we tried a thin one."

So, very carefully, the two creatures moved out along the thin branch. Suddenly, Edward halted.

"Avon! Look!"

From the opposite end of the very branch they were traveling on, another snail was coming toward them. What's more, there was not enough room for them to pass each other by. One of the snails would surely get knocked off.

Edward was very excited. He ran up and down and around in circles. "Avon," he said, "this is the adventure you have been waiting for. That snail is coming our direction. We are going his. One of you has to give way. You're going to fight a famous battle and win!"

"What if I lose?" asked Avon.

"Avon, if you win this battle, you will be the most famous snail in the world. This is what going on adventures is all about!"

"The truth is, Edward, I've never fought

a famous battle before. How do you do it?"

"Hurry down the branch and push him out of the way. He will push you back. Push him again. That's a battle."

No matter how Avon tried to explain that snails were not pushy creatures, Edward urged him on. So, with much reluctance, Avon set off down the branch. From the far end, the other snail kept coming.

Edward scrambled back to watch from a safe distance.

The two snails moved along the long branch a little bit at a time.

"Faster, faster!" urged Edward.

The two snails moved forward slowly.

"Don't take so long!" cried Edward.

The snails moved on, coming closer and closer.

"It's been two hours since you began!" shouted Edward, who, in spite of himself, was becoming a little bored.

"I'm going at top speed," said Avon.

By lunchtime the two snails had covered half the distance that had separated them.

"Can I stop for something to eat?" asked Avon.

"No, no, the matter is urgent," Edward insisted. "Keep going!"

By four o'clock in the afternoon, the snails had covered three-quarters of the distance.

Edward was exhausted with watching.

"Can't you go any faster?" he called.

"I'm running," replied Avon.

By suppertime the two snails were almost close.

"Remember, now," said Edward from his perch, "this is a fight to the finish." He yawned.

The two snails were almost touching when the sun went down.

"I can't see you anymore, Avon!" Edward called out. "Keep me informed."

When it had become completely dark, there was a long silence.

"What's happening?" asked Edward.

"I'm not sure," replied Avon.

"I can't hear anything."

"Neither can I," said Avon.

A few more hours passed.

"Avon?"

"Yes, Edward?"

"Are you . . . winning?"

"Can't . . . tell."

In the middle of the night, Edward called out across the darkness, "How is it going?"

"Pretty well."

"Are you winning now?"

"Won't know till daylight," Avon replied.

In the morning Edward strained to have a look. To his astonishment the two snails had passed each other, and each was continuing on his way.

Edward hurriedly caught up with Avon.

"Avon! What happened? Did you win your famous battle?"

Avon considered thoughtfully. "Edward," he said, "I don't know. It all happened so quickly."

CHAPTER EIGHT

In Which the Adventurers Get Somewhere

Two mornings later, Avon woke before Edward. While Edward continued to sleep, Avon looked around the place where they had stopped for the night. He had to admit that it was rather like his own neighborhood, even though they had traveled more than half the length of the branch. When Edward woke, Avon asked him about it.

Edward explained. "You see, Avon, it all depends on you. If *you* want it to be different, it will be different. Don't look at the world with your eyes but with your heart."

"But Edward," said Avon, suddenly alarmed, "I don't have eyes on my heart."

"I was speaking as a poet might speak. You can't have adventures without poetry."

"Oh, I do love poems, Edward. I remember my mother telling me a poem. It went this way: 'Jack Snail and Jill Snail went up a hill to fetch a pail; they took one step, and then another, and—'"

Edward interrupted. "That's not the kind of poetry I mean. What I mean is that you take a lot of words, put them together, and they tell you something. The whole point is that if you don't know where you are, the best thing to do is write a poem. All adventurers do that sort of thing. It's part of the job."

"Will it tell us where we're going?"

"If we're looking that way."

Avon took a long look around. "I think I have a poem to say," he announced.

"Go on then."

Avon closed his eyes, and recited:

"How I wonder why the air
Is the same here as it was there."

"Bravo!" Edward clapped. "*Now* do you know where you are?"

"Well," said Avon, "I have narrowed it down to two places."

"Where?"

"Here or there."

"Good," said Edward. "You've got to start somewhere."

CHAPTER NINE

In Which Avon Does a Good Deed

A day later Avon and Edward came upon a caterpillar busily building a cocoon.

"That's the oddest house I ever saw," said Avon. "I don't think it will last very long—it's nothing but silky string. The first puff of wind will just blow it away."

Paying the two adventurers no attention, the caterpillar worked steadily on, never once stopping until she was through.

"I'd be a bit worried if I were going to stay there," Avon said to the caterpillar. "It's so flimsy, anyone might break in, or it might even fall apart. How long do you expect to be stopping here?"

"A month," replied the caterpillar.

"Coming and going, I suppose."

"No, just sleeping."

"The whole time?"

"Yes indeed," said the caterpillar, and she yawned.

Avon made up his mind at once. "I'm going to stand guard outside your house while you sleep," he announced.

"That's very kind of you," said the caterpillar, "but I'm sure—"

Avon interrupted. "No, I won't be put off. I'm going to do it. Adventurers are supposed to protect creatures."

"I really don't think it's necessary," insisted the caterpillar, "but you're free to do as you wish." Crawling into her new house, she closed the door behind her.

"I'd better check the windows and doors," said Avon. He went about making sure all was secure. "Things are just fine," he told Edward. "No one will trouble her."

They stayed there for a month, Avon constantly checking the house.

Each morning Edward asked Avon how the night had gone.

"Nothing happened," said Avon.

"I'm impressed," said Edward, "with how much you're getting done."

One month from the day the caterpillar had gone into her house, Avon heard some sounds from the inside.

"Edward," he called, "I think the caterpillar is waking up! She's going to come out." Dashing around, he did a final check to make sure things were in proper order, then went by the door to wait. As he waited, he said, "Edward, you'll have to admit I've done a good job."

"Avon," said Edward in sincere admiration, "you have been wonderful."

"I do think," said Avon, "I can truly say that this has been an adventure at last!"

"Quite right," agreed Edward. "We might be able to go home immediately."

The door of the cocoon opened a little bit. Avon peered around to get a better look but couldn't see anything. Slowly the door swung open and out came...a *butterfly*.

The butterfly walked to the edge of a leaf and fanned her wings.

Avon was astonished. Edward was speechless.

Avon looked into the house to see if perhaps the caterpillar was still there. When he saw that the cocoon was empty, he rushed over to the butterfly.

"What have you done with the caterpillar?" he cried.

The butterfly looked curiously at Avon. "Were you speaking to me?" she asked.

"There was a caterpillar in there," Avon said.

"I am afraid," said the butterfly in a haughty tone, "that I don't know what you are talking about. As you can plainly see, *I* am a butterfly. I have nothing to do with caterpillars."

Before Avon could ask another question, she flew away.

Avon felt so bad, he almost cried.

"I didn't do very well," he confessed.

Edward was glum. "It looks that way."

"What do you think I did wrong?"

"As far as I can tell, you did nothing."

"I promise you," said Avon with a shake of his head, "that the next time I do nothing, I'll do it better. But I guess we can't quit."

"I'm afraid not, Avon. Not now, anyway."

So they started off again.

CHAPTER TEN

In Which the Adventurers Come to an End

The two adventurers were going along.
Avon was singing:

> "*March, march*
> *Golly, golly, golly.*
> *March, march*
> *Golly, golly—*"

"Stop!" cried Edward.

"Are you referring to my speed or my song?" Avon asked.

"Look what's there," said Edward, pointing straight ahead.

"I don't see a thing."

"Exactly. We've reached the end of the branch."

"Good heavens," said Avon. "I hadn't noticed. I might have fallen off."

With great care the two creatures edged to the very tip. From there they looked out at the cloudless sky.

"The end of the branch," said Avon, mostly to himself.

"The beginning of the sky," said Edward, mostly to *himself*.

"Which is it?" asked Avon. "The beginning or the end?"

"I should think," said Edward, "it depends on what there's more of, the tree or the sky. How long did it take us to get here?"

"All my life," said Avon.

Edward nodded. "It's a very long branch, then. How long would it take to climb the sky?"

"I can't tell," confessed Avon. "I've never done it."

"Use your brain, Avon. Think of all the things that get in your way along the branch—leaves, bark, other creatures, a million things to slow you down. Now look at the sky."

Avon looked. "There's nothing there."

"Exactly. So it's bound to take less time."

"I see your point."

"Which means," continued Edward, "that it will take *longer* to climb the branch. And if it takes longer, the branch must be bigger. And if the branch is bigger than the sky, that means we're at sky's end, but only at the beginning of the branch."

"You mean," asked Avon, quite amazed, "that after all this time, we're just *beginning*?"

"Worse," Edward pointed out. "Since this is the beginning, if we hadn't gotten to this point, we would not have begun."

"Oh goodness," said Avon. "All that traveling, and we haven't even started. I had no idea how far you have to go before you can start. Almost makes me want to stop."

"You can't do that, either," said Edward severely.

"Why?"

"Can't very well stop if you haven't started, can you?"

"Edward," cried Avon, "I never knew how important it was to start before you begin."

And turning around, they began.

CHAPTER ELEVEN

In Which a Cricket Is Helped

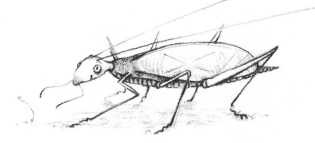

C̶ik, cik, cik, cik, cik, cik."

"What's that?" asked Avon.

"A cricket," explained Edward. "Isn't it irritating the way all crickets sing the same song? That's the trouble with most crea-tures. They have no creativity. They do the same thing, the same way, day in, day out, from parent to child, without ever doing anything differently."

"My father never wanted to seek adventures," said Avon.

"What did he do?"

"He wrote about fast food for *Reader's Digestion*."

Edward went up to the cricket and said, "I beg your pardon, but that song—where did you find it?"

The cricket was bewildered. "It's what all crickets sing."

"Surely," said Edward, "you are not just the same as all the other crickets, are you?"

"I've never given it much thought," said the cricket.

"Now's your opportunity," announced

Edward. "I'm a creative songwriter. What sorts of things interest you in particular?"

"Now that you mention it," said the cricket, "I'm ever so fond of cheese."

"Good job!" said Edward. "What you clearly need is a cheese song. Avon, you and the cricket have yourselves a chat. I'm going off to write a song."

Two hours later Edward came back.

"I've worked up a beautiful cheese song," he told the cricket. "I've used your melody, but the words are my own creation." Edward cleared his throat and sang, "*'Cheese, cheese, cheese, cheese, cheese.'*"

"That's it exactly," said the cricket. "That's exactly the way I feel about cheese."

"Give it a try," suggested Edward.

The cricket sang, "*'Cheese, cheese, cheese, cheese...'*" Just as he was about to conclude the song, a bird swooped down and tried to gobble him up. Fortunately, the bird missed.

The cricket was very upset. "If I sing that song," he cried, "I'll be so different from all other crickets that every bird in the world will know where I am and try to eat me."

"I suggest you sing it in your house, then," said Edward.

"But if I do that," protested the cricket, "no one will hear me."

"Better and better," said Edward. "Have you ever *never* heard a cricket?"

"True enough," said Avon. "Every cricket I ever heard I could listen to."

"Precisely," agreed Edward. "You," he said to the cricket, "will be the one-in-the-world cricket who, when creatures listen, won't be heard."

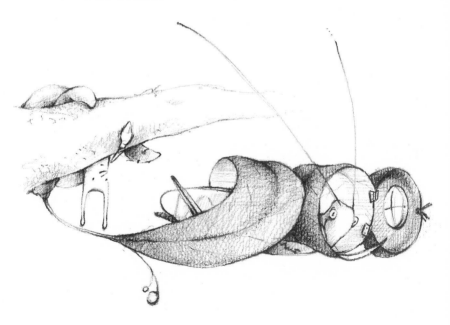

Excited by the idea, the cricket hurried to his house, shut the door, and began to sing.

Nothing could be heard.

"Gosh," mused Avon, "being creative *does* make a difference."

And the two adventurers continued on their way.

CHAPTER
TWELVE

In Which Avon Does Some Writing

It was late at night, and Edward was almost asleep, when Avon called across the dark.

"Do you realize," said Avon, "that in all the time we have been traveling, I have not written one letter. No, not even a postcard."

"You could start now," suggested Edward. "Is there someone you want to write to?"

"I'm afraid not," said Avon.

"Yes," agreed Edward, "writing a letter is easy enough. It's deciding whom to send it to that's the hard part. Have you any friends?"

"You."

"Why not write to me, then?"

"Would you mind?"

"I should say not. It's wonderful to hear from friends when they're traveling."

"I'll do it, then," said Avon. "Good night, Edward."

"Good night, Avon."

Taking out pencil and paper, Avon wrote: *Dear Edward.* Then he thought for a long time about what to write next. Not getting on very well, he called out, "Edward?"

"Yes, Avon."

"What sorts of things do you like to hear about in letters?"

"Oh," said Edward, "something interesting, unusual. You know, I would just like to learn how you're getting on."

"Oh, fine. Good night, Edward."

"Good night, Avon."

Looking across the paper, Avon realized there wasn't very much room to write all the things that were of interest to Edward.

"Edward!" he called.

"Yes, Avon."

"I don't have much room here. Of all the things you said you liked to read about, is there *one* in particular you would find *most* interesting?"

"Most of all," said Edward, "I'd like to know what you're doing."

"Oh, well," said Avon, "that's easy enough. Good night, Edward."

"Good night, Avon."

Avon wrote: *I am writing you a letter.* It took up just about all the paper.

"Edward?"

"Yes, Avon."

"In the letters you get, what kind of salutation do you like at the end?"

"Avon, a salutation comes at the beginning. What comes at the end is a closing."

"Thank you," said Avon. "That brings a conclusion to my confusion. But I still want to be open about closings. So do you prefer... *Yours truly, Sincerely yours,* or *Best regards*?"

Without a moment's hesitation, Edward

said, *"Yours sincerely."*

"Why?"

"It's...sincere."

"Edward?"

"Yes, Avon."

"Would you mind very much listening to the letter so I could get your opinion of it?"

"Not at all."

Avon read the letter: *"Dear Edward, I am writing you a letter. Yours sincerely, Avon."*

"An excellent letter, Avon," said Edward. "It tells me everything you're doing."

"I'll mail it tomorrow morning," said Avon. "You should get it in a few days."

"Wonderful," said Edward. "There's nothing better than coming home from a

long trip and finding a letter waiting for
you. It brings you right up to date with your
friends."

"Good night, Edward."

"Good night, Avon."

CHAPTER
THIRTEEN

In Which the Adventurers
Find a Puzzle

*O*hhhhhh."

Avon and Edward stopped to listen.

"*Ohhhhhh.*"

"It sounds like a creature in trouble," whispered Avon.

"Be calm," said Edward, who had found a good place to listen behind Avon's back.

"I think we should help," said Avon.

"That's what they do in the books. It's sure to be a thrilling adventure."

"Never rush into anything which may want rushing out of," cautioned Edward. "If the sound comes again, I may be able to tell you something more."

"Ohhhhhh."

"What is it?" Avon asked in a hushed tone.

Edward considered. "It's something going, *'Ohhhhhh.'*"

"Can you tell what the matter is?"

"No, only what it's saying."

"Ohhhhhh."

"It's right over there!" cried Avon, becoming more and more impatient. "This is my big chance."

"It may be a warning to keep away!" shouted Edward, but it was too late. Avon was heading directly over to the other side of the branch. Edward followed slowly.

When they got there, they found a worm curled up in almost a complete circle so that its two ends were nearly touching.

"Ohhhhhh," moaned the worm. The sound didn't come from one end or the other but from somewhere in the middle.

Speaking to neither end, Avon asked, "Were you calling for help?"

"Oh dear, oh dear," said the worm. "Yes, perhaps you can help me. I went to sleep, but when I woke up, I had forgotten which end of me was the front and which end the back. I don't know which is the beginning and which the end!" he wailed.

Avon was astonished.

"No clues?" asked Edward, who had remained calm.

"Can *you* tell which end is which?" asked the worm, a bit vexed.

"No, I can't," admitted Avon.

Edward thought for a moment. Then he picked up a tiny bit of leaf and waved it through the air. "What I suggest," he said, "is that I tickle one of your ends and then the other. Whichever end sneezes should be your nose. With that as a start, we should be able to make a good guess of things, putting an end to your problem."

"But my problem *is* my end," said the worm. "Besides, I'm terribly ticklish."

Edward became cross. "Now see here, Worm. Pull yourself together. This is no laughing matter. It's not we who have lost our wits. If we can't help, you are doomed to a life without an end."

The severity of Edward's tone calmed the worm. And when he considered what the ant had said, he realized how helpful Edward was trying to be. "I'm ready," the worm said grimly.

Like a careful doctor, Edward applied the leaf bit to one end of the worm.

Nothing happened.

Edward stepped back, frowning. "I'll give it a try on the other end. If I'm wrong this time, I'm afraid we are in for an unhappy ending."

Avon was so tense, he looked the other way.

Edward applied the leaf bit again.

The worm sneezed.

"Sir," said Edward, pointing dramatically, "*that* is your beginning and *that* is your end."

"Thank you," said the worm, "for putting an end to my troubles."

The two adventurers once again set off.

"That was wonderful, Edward," said Avon. "You were ever so confident."

"It just looked that way," confessed Edward. "I don't mind telling you, I was worried for a moment. It worked out, but a situation like that can cause complications which can go on forever."

"You mean...endless?"

"Exactly."

CHAPTER
FOURTEEN

In Which Avon Sings

I've such a terrible memory," said Avon as he and Edward were going along.

"What have you forgotten?" asked Edward.

"That's just it," said Avon. "I'm not sure at all. Have you any ideas?"

"Perhaps you were trying to remember that song I wrote for the cricket. You know, the one with the catchy lyrics. Was that it?"

"Exactly!" exclaimed Avon. "I was trying to sing it to myself, but all I could remember were the first four words. You know, *'Cheese, cheese, cheese, cheese...'* There, you see, I've forgotten the rest."

Edward sang it through. *"'Cheese, cheese, cheese, cheese, cheese.'"*

"Right," said Avon, and he sang the song. *"'Cheese, cheese, cheese, cheese, cheese.'"*

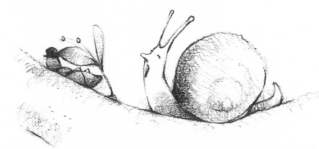

"You *do* have a bad memory," said Edward. "You've got the words all right, but now you've mixed them up. It goes this way: *'Cheese, cheese, cheese, cheese, cheese.'*"

"I've got it now," said Avon, and he tried it again. "*'Cheese, cheese, cheese, cheese, cheese.'* Is that it?"

"Close enough."

CHAPTER FIFTEEN

*In Which the Adventurers
Enter a Curious House*

It was in the afternoon that Avon and Edward came upon a house.

Avon stared at it for a long time. "How strange," he said. "We've traveled so far, and yet there's a house which seems just like my own."

Edward became excited. "Avon," he whispered, "this may very well be a magic house."

"And look," cried Avon, "here's something even stranger! Not only does this house remind me of my own, back where we came from, but here is a sign which says, 'Avon Snail.'"

"Avon," said Edward breathlessly, "this is not just magic but *powerful* magic!"

With extreme caution, the two creatures pushed open the door and peered into the house.

Avon became more astonished. "It even *looks* like the inside of my house."

"Do you notice anything else odd?" Edward wanted to know.

"The tables and chairs," said Avon, "are

just the way I like them. Even the pictures on
the wall are to my fancy. Oh, Edward, someone has gone to a great deal of trouble."

"It's perfectly clear to me," said Edward. "Now I know why we have had so many extraordinary adventures. All the time, traveling right along with us, was an invisible magician."

"An invisible magician," said Avon, surprised. "How stupid of me never to have noticed."

"This house proves I am right," said Edward. "No doubt that invisible magician took an old castle and turned it into a house which you would like."

"I'm grateful and flattered," said Avon.

Edward snorted. "Nonsense. It has nothing to do with kindness. He owes it to you!"

"I don't see why."

"Avon, just how many snails do you know who believe in magic adventures?"

"Just myself—and you—but, of course, you're not a snail."

"Exactly," said Edward. "The invisible magician is merely showing his gratitude for your believing."

Suddenly, Avon felt very happy. "Just think," he said, "to go on a long trip, to come so far from where you live, and then— then to come upon a magic castle which has all the comforts of home. Oh, Edward, this has been the most exciting adventure of all. I believe I am happy at last."

Edward nodded and said, "I've always believed a man's castle should be his home."

CHAPTER
SIXTEEN

In Which an Adventure Is Added

Avon and Edward decided to remain in the magic castle and live there together. Avon had become very famous for his adventures. Creatures from all over the neighborhood came to visit him.

His old friend the newt came. "What was your most exciting adventure?" he asked.

Avon turned to Edward for help. "Which

one should I tell him?"

Edward considered the question in his usual thoughtful way. "Tell him about your great race with the grasshopper."

Avon was about to tell that adventure to the newt when he remembered just in time that he never did have a race with a grasshopper.

"Don't worry, Avon," said Edward. "If it never really happened, there's not much danger of telling it wrong. Now that you're famous, you don't want to say the wrong thing."

"Maybe I should sing it?"

"Better write than song," said Edward.

So Avon wrote out his "Great Grasshopper Race Adventure." When he was
done, he read it aloud:

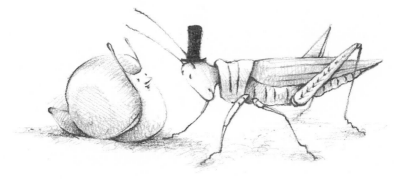

"One day a grasshopper challenged
Avon to a race.

'Sure,' said Avon. 'But where will we
race to?'

'I suggest,' said the grasshopper, 'we
go from here to there.'

Avon thought about it. Then he said,
'Does it matter which direction we go?'

'As long as it's between here and
there,' returned the grasshopper, 'I
suppose it will be the same distance.'

'In that case,' said Avon with a smile,
'I suggest we race from there to here.'

'That's fine with me,' the grasshopper
agreed, 'but why would you want to do it
that way?'

'Well,' said Avon, 'if we race from
there to here—instead of from here
to there—since I'm already here and
you're there—I win.' "

CHAPTER
SEVENTEEN

In Which the Adventures Conclude

When Avon had finished, the newt shook his head in admiration.

"Lad," he said, "that's the kind of story that makes me want to go out and have my own adventures. In fact, I'm leaving immediately."

"Good luck!" Avon called as the newt left.

A grinning Avon turned to Edward.

"You know, Edward, even though it never happened, I think *that* was the best adventure of all. And the newt seemed to find it very moving."

"He certainly left right away," said Edward. "I particularly liked the part about being here. It confirmed what I've come to believe: You're a hero."

Avon blushed. "You're right. I would rather be here than anywhere. Edward, you've helped me come a long way."

"I'm glad I was helpful," said Edward. "Though, most of all, I'm pleased by the way your adventures allowed our friendship to begin. But now that's done."

Avon grew alarmed. "Edward, are you

suggesting our friendship is ending?"

"I rather think," said the ant, "it's just the end of the beginning."

"But, Edward," Avon cried out, "that means—"

"What?"

"We've never had a middle."

"Oh, never mind," said Edward. "Next time we have an adventure, we'll start in the middle."

"And then," said Avon, "we can go in any direction we want."

Edward thought for a long time. Then he said, "You're right. That's the *only* way to go."

The End

(of the Beginning)